This
MOUSE WORKS
Classics Collection Storybook
belongs to

Disney's HERCULES

CLASSIC STORYBOOK

WALT DISNEY PICTURES PRESENTS "HERCULES" MUSIC BY ALAN MENKEN LYRICS BY DAVID ZIPPEL ORIGINAL SCORE BY ALAN MENKEN
SCREENPLAY BY RON CLEMENTS & JOHN MUSKER, BOB SHAW & DON McENERY AND IRENE MECCHI
PRODUCED BY ALICE DEWEY AND JOHN MUSKER & RON CLEMENTS DIRECTED BY JOHN MUSKER & RON CLEMENTS
DISTRIBUTED BY BUENA VISTA PICTURES DISTRIBUTION, INC. © DISNEY ENTERPRISES, INC.

MOUSE WORKS

Also available in Spanish

Adapted by Lisa Ann Marsoli
Penciled by Judith Holmes Clarke, Denise Shimabukuro, and Scott Tilley
Painted by Atelier Philippe Harchy
Printed in the United States of America
ISBN: 1-57082-518-1
1 3 5 7 9 10 8 6 4 2

Pay attention! Yes, we're talkin' to you.
Perhaps you've seen us on a vase or two?
We're the Muses, and you won't believe
The fantastic story that's up our sleeve.

Long ago, when the world was just made,
Some horrible Titans made the people afraid.
Volcanoes erupted, there were storms and earthquakes—
The earth was a mess, but, hey! Those are the breaks!

Then the boss-man, Zeus, threw those guys in a hole.
To make order from chaos was his ultimate goal.
He assigned each god and goddess a job to do,
And the people were grateful—their troubles were few!
But one day something happened way up on high
That would change history in the blink of an eye...

Fireworks lit up the sky over Mount Olympus, home of the gods, to celebrate the arrival of Zeus and Hera's son, Hercules. It was obvious to everyone that this was no ordinary baby. He was cute and cuddly, to be sure, but also unbelievably strong. Why, he could easily lift his mighty father above his head!

All the Olympian gods attended the celebration, bringing an array of amazing presents. But Zeus was not to be outdone. He spun several clouds into an adorable winged baby horse as a present to Baby Hercules from himself and Hera. "His name is Pegasus, and he's all yours, Son," Zeus said, beaming.

Soon, Hades, the god of the Underworld, appeared. He hated Zeus for putting him in charge of a place that was full of dead people. But Zeus was Hades' boss, after all, so Hades just smiled sweetly and handed Baby Hercules a pacifier—shaped like a skeleton.

Baby Hercules grabbed Hades' hand and squeezed it until Hades reeled in pain. "He's going to be the strongest of all the gods," Zeus announced proudly.

Hades quickly left the party on Olympus and headed back to the Underworld, his temper—and his hair—flaring. He was making plans for the day when he would overthrow Zeus and rule the universe.

When he docked at the Underworld, his two henchmen, Pain and Panic, told him that the Fates had arrived.

The Fates were three hideous old women who could see the past, present, and future with the one eye they shared. They were in charge of cutting a person's Thread of Life, sending each one straight to the Underworld.

"So, is this Hercules kid gonna mess up my plan to take over Olympus, or what?" an anxious Hades asked them. They refused to say, so Hades resorted to flattery. "Did you get your hair cut? Get a makeover? You look fabulous!" he told the shriveled old crones.

The Fates relented, telling Hades that in eighteen years, when the planets became perfectly aligned, Hades could indeed overthrow Zeus. "But," they added, "if Hercules fights on the side of the gods, you will fail."

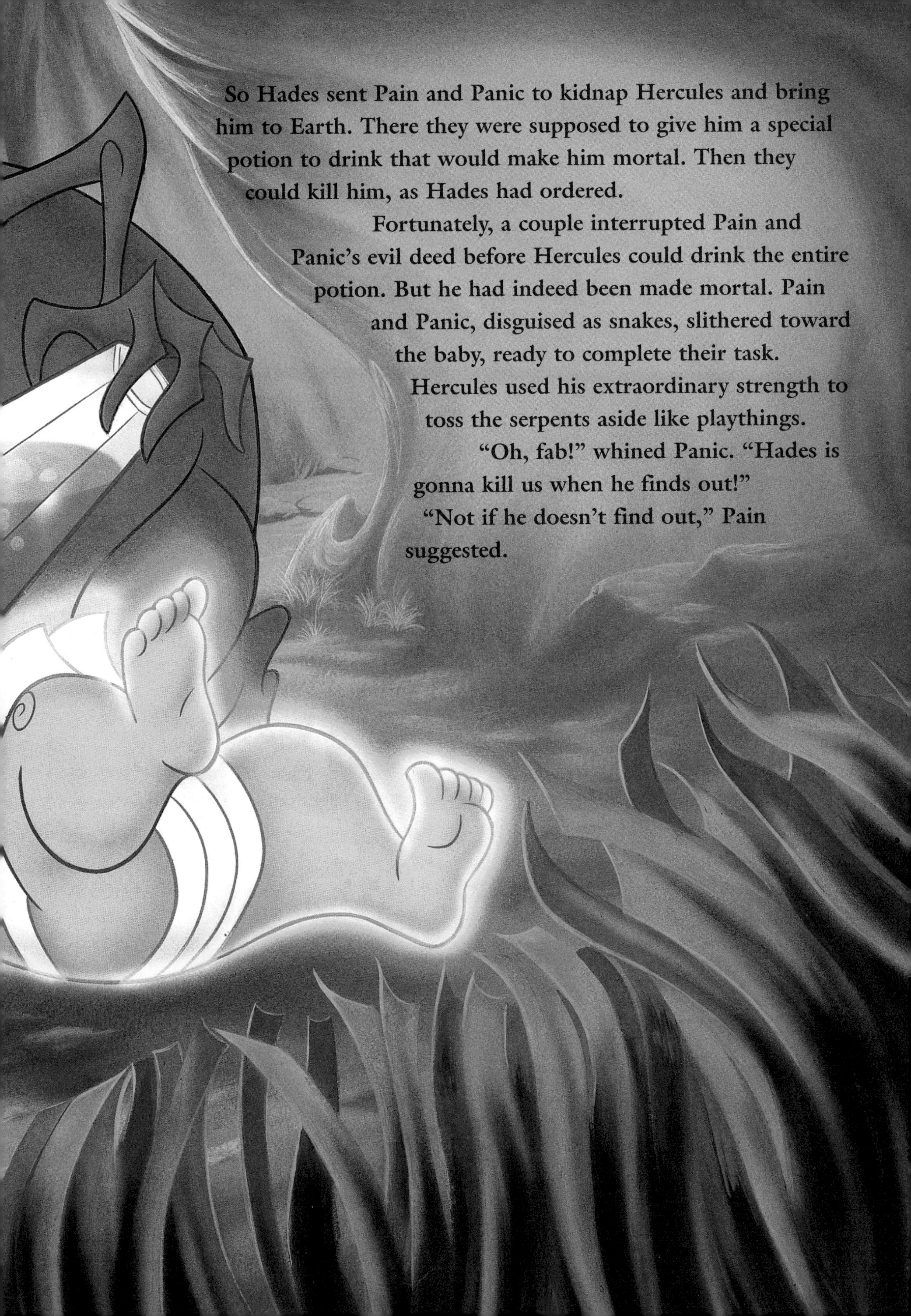

So Hades sent Pain and Panic to kidnap Hercules and bring him to Earth. There they were supposed to give him a special potion to drink that would make him mortal. Then they could kill him, as Hades had ordered.

Fortunately, a couple interrupted Pain and Panic's evil deed before Hercules could drink the entire potion. But he had indeed been made mortal. Pain and Panic, disguised as snakes, slithered toward the baby, ready to complete their task.

Hercules used his extraordinary strength to toss the serpents aside like playthings.

"Oh, fab!" whined Panic. "Hades is gonna kill us when he finds out!"

"Not if he doesn't find out," Pain suggested.

Now that Hercules was mortal, he could not return to Olympus. Zeus and Hera could only watch sadly from above as their baby was adopted by the childless couple, Amphitryon and Alcmene.

Under his adopted parents' loving care, Hercules grew into a devoted son. He tried to use his great strength to help out—like the time he replaced their donkey, Penelope, when she became lame on the way to the marketplace. Unfortunately, he usually wasn't able to control his strength. People avoided Hercules because, wherever he went, disaster often followed.

For example, one day in the marketplace, Hercules wanted to join some of the boys in a game of discus.

"Sorry, Herc. We've already got five, and we want to keep it an even number," they said, clumsily turning him down.

Nevertheless, the eager Hercules ran after their discus, knocking into the pillars of the marketplace and leaving it in ruins. The townspeople had enough, and warned his father to keep him away.

"I'll never fit in around here!" Hercules lamented.

Hercules knew there had to be someplace where he would fit in—where he wouldn't feel like an outsider.

He told his parents he had to find out where he belonged. They decided the time was right to show him the gold medallion he had been wearing when they found him.

"It has the symbol of the gods on it," Alcmene explained.

"Maybe they have the answers I'm looking for," Hercules mused. Now he knew he should begin his quest at the temple of Zeus. With heavy hearts, Hercules and his parents bid each other good-bye.

At the temple, as Hercules knelt before the enormous statue of Zeus to pray, the statue came to life.

"EEEEOWW!" screamed Hercules, running away from the giant figure.

"Hey, hold on, kiddo! Is that the kind of hello you give your father?" Zeus asked him.

Hercules was confused! If Zeus was his father, then Hercules must be a god.

But Zeus explained that Hercules wasn't a god, he was human now—and humans were not allowed on Olympus.

"You mean you can't do a thing?" Hercules asked in despair.

"I can't, but you can," Zeus explained. "You must prove yourself a true hero on Earth," Zeus told him. "Begin by seeking out Philoctetes, the trainer of heroes, on the Isle of Idra." Then, to help him on his way, Zeus reunited Hercules with his old pal Pegasus.

"I won't let you down, Father!" called Hercules as he and Pegasus flew off toward Idra.

Hercules was surprised to discover that Philoctetes was a wisecracking little satyr—a half-man, half-goat creature, complete with horns. Hercules told Phil about his dream of being a hero and asked the trainer to help him.

"I had a dream once, too—that I was gonna train the greatest hero there ever was!" Phil declared. "So great, the gods would hang a picture of him in the stars." Then Phil explained that everyone he had ever tried to help had disappointed him—especially Achilles. "Now there was a guy who had it all! The build, the foot speed...he could keep on coming. But that furshlugginer heel of his! Dreams are for rookies," he continued. "A guy can only take so much disappointment."

Hercules tried to convince Phil that he was special by demonstrating his remarkable strength. "I'm different from those other guys!" Hercules insisted. "I can go the distance!" He even revealed to Phil that he was the son of Zeus.

"Zeus? The big guy?" asked Phil in disbelief. "Mr. Lightning Bolts?"

Hercules swore it was the truth, yet Phil still refused—until Zeus sent a lightning bolt his way.

"Okay!" Phil agreed, convinced. "You win!"

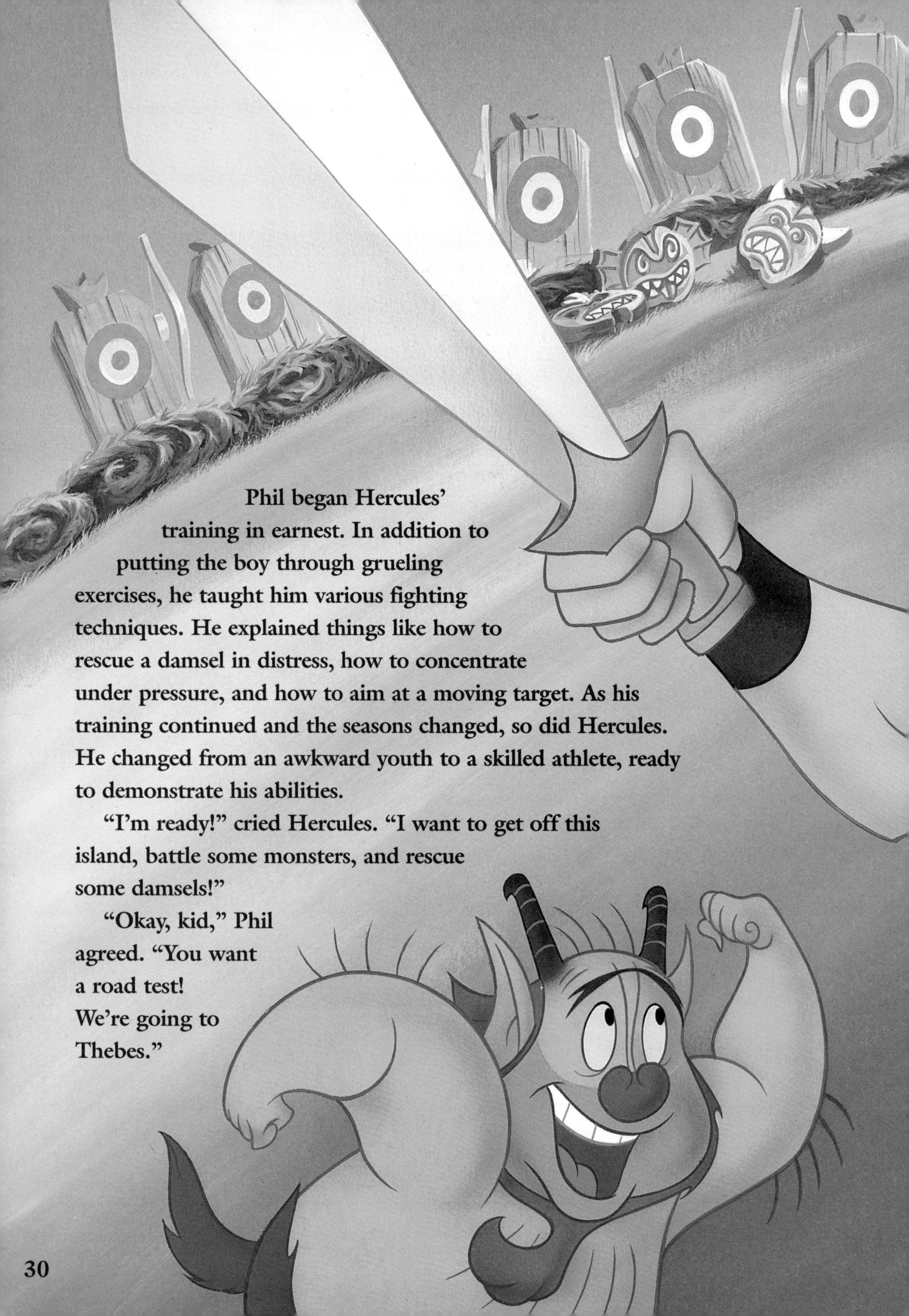

Phil began Hercules' training in earnest. In addition to putting the boy through grueling exercises, he taught him various fighting techniques. He explained things like how to rescue a damsel in distress, how to concentrate under pressure, and how to aim at a moving target. As his training continued and the seasons changed, so did Hercules. He changed from an awkward youth to a skilled athlete, ready to demonstrate his abilities.

"I'm ready!" cried Hercules. "I want to get off this island, battle some monsters, and rescue some damsels!"

"Okay, kid," Phil agreed. "You want a road test! We're going to Thebes."

On the way to Thebes, they came upon Meg, a beautiful and self-assured young woman who was in the clutches of a burly centaur named Nessus.

"Back off, Atlas," Meg snapped at Hercules when he tried to help. But Hercules—eager to rack up hero points—fought with the centaur anyway.

Hercules won, even though Phil wasn't too crazy about his fighting technique.

With Nessus out of the picture, Hercules tried to introduce himself to Meg, but he became shy and tongue-tied.

Phil didn't like all the attention Hercules was paying to her. After all, a hero shouldn't have any distractions. Pegasus wasn't crazy about this gal, either. In fact, he was downright jealous! When Hercules offered Meg a ride, the horse flew up into a tree.

"I'll be all right," Meg assured Hercules as she walked off. "I can tie my own sandals and everything. Bye-bye, Wonder Boy."

But now Meg was in trouble. She had to explain to her boss, Hades, that some strongman named Hercules had chased the centaur off and she wasn't able to recruit him.

Hades became inflamed when he heard that Hercules was alive! "Dead as a doornail," he spat at Pain and Panic. "Weren't those your exact words?" Hades grabbed his henchmen by their long, slithery tails.

"At least we made him mortal," they stammered.

So Hades hatched a plot to get rid of Hercules once and for all.

Meanwhile, in Thebes, Hercules announced that he was the hero for them. The Thebans just rolled their eyes. No hero had ever been able to stop the fires, earthquakes, and floods that had plagued them.

"You'll get your chance," Phil told him. "All we need is a catastrophe."

Right on cue, Meg appeared. "Two little boys are trapped by a rock slide!" she cried. Hercules was thrilled. This was his chance!

As the townsfolk crowded around the edge of the canyon, Hercules lifted a massive boulder high over his head, freeing the boys. Hercules waited, but only a few people applauded. The Thebans were a tough audience! The boys scampered up the canyon. They stopped at Hades' feet and changed back into Pain and Panic.

Moments later, Phil joined Hercules in the canyon, and the two became aware of a weird hissing sound.

Suddenly there was a crack of lightning, and a gigantic dragonlike creature—the Hydra—emerged from the mouth of a cave. Phil ran for cover while Hercules, sword drawn, battled the beast until it threw him into the air and swallowed him whole.

But after a moment, Hercules slashed his way out of the monster's throat and sent its head toppling to the ground.

Pain and Panic stole nervous glances at Hades, but the hotheaded god was strangely relaxed. For the Hydra was not dead. Three writhing heads emerged from a wound in her neck. Hercules, atop Pegasus, sliced at them with his sword, but each time he did, they multiplied!

"Forget the head-slicing thing!" Phil coached. "It's not working!"

Finally the enormous creature pinned Hercules to a cliff with a claw. Thinking quickly, Hercules smashed his fist into the mountain, causing an avalanche that buried him and the Hydra under a mountain of rocks. But then Hercules shocked everyone by emerging from the Hydra's claw unharmed!

Hold the phone, we just gotta break in!
This is where Herc's fame and fortune begin.
From that day on he had battles galore...
Boars, harpies, sea monsters, lions, and more!
He had gone from a nothing, a no one, a zero,
To a champion, a star, a celebrity hero!
Fans and groupies cheered wherever he went.
Did we mention his handprints got put in cement?

Even Pain and Panic couldn't resist the Hercules-mania sweeping the land. During a "get Hercules" strategy session, Hades noticed that Pain was wearing a new pair of Hercules sandals, and Panic was slurping on a cup of "Herculade" sports drink.

Hades started burning up. "I've got twenty-four hours to get rid of this bozo or the entire scheme I've been setting up for eighteen years goes up in smoke...AND YOU'RE WEARING HIS MERCHANDISE!" he shrieked.

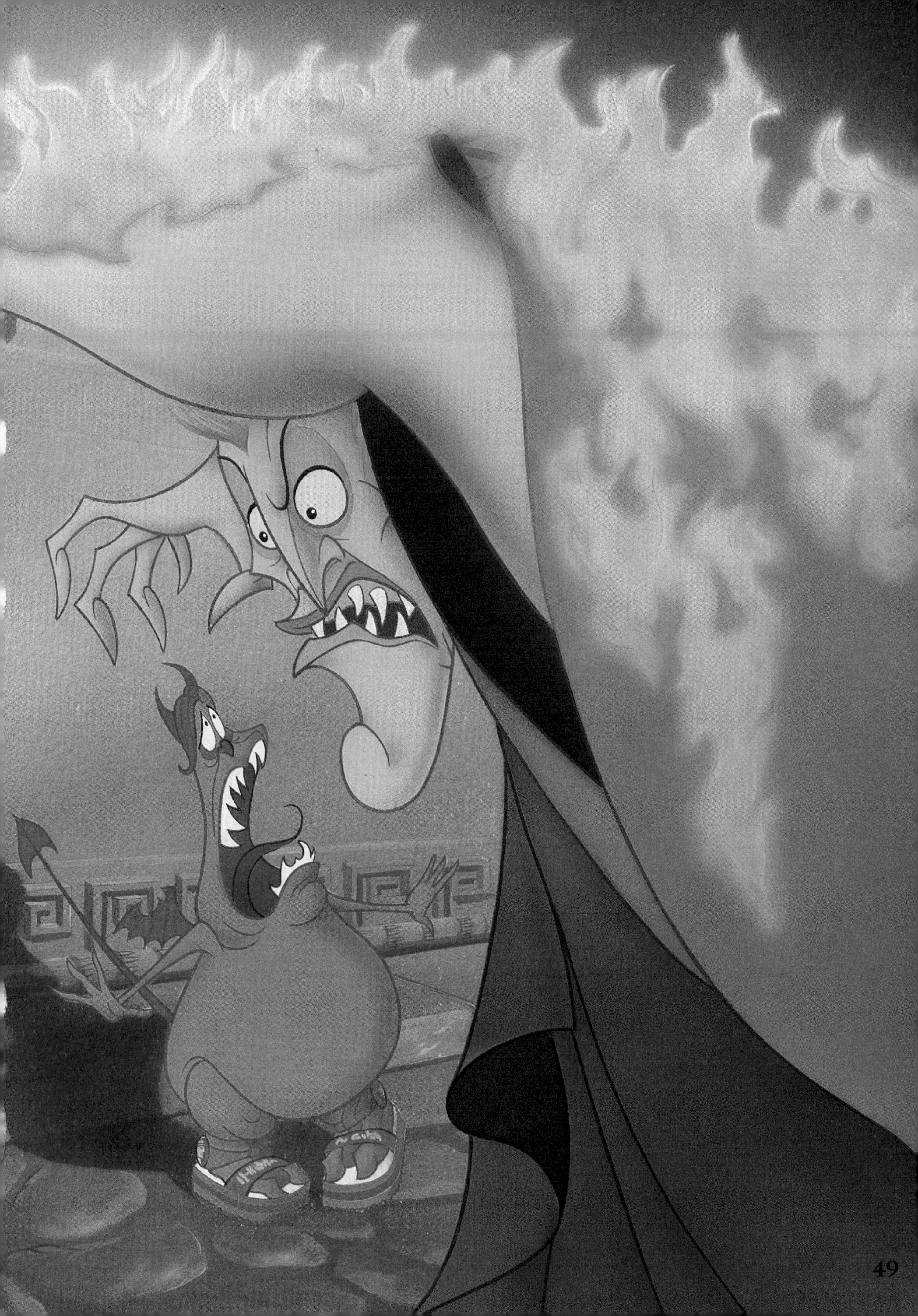

Hades cooled down. “He’s got to have a weakness,” he said. “For Pandora, it was the box thing. The Trojans bet on the wrong horse...”

Hades knew Meg could get close enough to Hercules to discover his weakness. Then Hades could use it to destroy him. Meg refused, but she had once made a deal with Hades, trading her freedom to save her ex-boyfriend’s life. Now she had to do what Hades wanted. To sweeten the deal, Hades promised to release her if she succeeded.

Meanwhile, Hercules visited Zeus at the temple, reenacting some of his victories for his adoring father. But Zeus gently broke the news that Hercules was still not ready to rejoin the other gods on Mount Olympus.

"I'm the most famous person in all of Greece!" Hercules protested. "I mean, I'm an action figure!"

"My boy, I'm afraid that being famous isn't the same as being a true hero," Zeus explained. "Look inside your heart to discover what you must do."

Later, back at Hercules' villa, Phil ran down the list of the day's activities while Hercules posed for a vase painting. "...at noon ya got a luncheon with the Daughters of the Greek Revolution...at one ya got a meeting with King Augeus..."

But Hercules seemed distracted. "This isn't getting me anywhere," he sighed to Phil. "I'll never make it to Olympus."

They were interrupted when a group of Hercules' admirers burst into the room. Hercules hid while Phil herded the fans out, but one girl stayed behind. Hercules was thrilled to discover it was Meg.

"So," Meg wondered, "you look like you could use a break. Think your nanny goat would go berserk if you played hooky this afternoon?"

Hercules gladly ignored his duties as a celebrity, and the two went off to spend the day together. Meg questioned Hercules to discover his weaknesses, but realized he had none. Though she would not admit it to herself, Meg found herself falling in love.

When Phil caught up with them that evening he was hopping mad! Hercules reluctantly left for home, though he was so starry-eyed that he didn't even notice when Phil fell off Pegasus.

Phil was grumbling and trying to free himself from a briar patch when he overheard voices. Peering through the bushes, he saw Hades talking to Meg. Suddenly, he realized that Meg had been working for Hades all along.

"I knew that dame was trouble. This is gonna break the kid's heart," Phil said to himself as he raced off to tell Hercules the truth.

What was even worse was that Hades had discovered that Hercules did have a weakness—and that weakness was Meg.

When Phil found Hercules at the stadium, the young hero couldn't stop talking about how wonderful Meg was.

"Isn't she the brightest, funniest, most amazing girl you ever met?" Hercules gushed.

"Sure, but she's also a fraud," Phil insisted. "The whole thing is some kinda set-up!"

When Hercules became furious and refused to believe him, Phil told Hercules he was on his own. "I thought you were gonna be the all-time champ...not the all-time chump!" the trainer fumed. Saddened by Hercules' stubbornness, Phil left him alone to brood.

While Phil and Hercules were arguing, Pain and Panic went to work. The two transformed themselves into a beautiful female horse and pranced in front of Pegasus. Always a sucker for a pretty mane, Pegasus followed the filly into a nearby stable. But talk about a bad date—within seconds, his mare dissolved and changed back into Pain and Panic. Hades' henchmen tied Pegasus up and left him inside, unable to help Hercules should he need him.

Hercules would need him, and soon. As the alignment of the planets approached, Hades was becoming desperate. He went to the stadium to plead his case to Hercules. He tried to play it cool—which was very hard for such a hotheaded guy to do.

"I would be eternally grateful if you would just take one day off from this hero business of yours," Hades said casually. "I mean, monsters, natural disasters...they can wait a day, okay?"

Suspecting that people would get hurt, Hercules refused—until Hades revealed Meg, bound at his side.

Now Hercules was forced to make a deal. If Hercules would give up his strength for one day, Hades promised that Meg would be safe. Hercules agreed. Then, when his strength was gone, Hades revealed that Meg had been working for him all along. Hercules faced the awful truth, weak and heartbroken.

When at last the planets aligned, Hades could free the Titans from their underground prison. “Brothers!” Hades bellowed. “Who locked you away in this prison? And if I let you out, what’s the first thing you’re gonna do?”

“Destroy him! Destroy Zeus!” thundered the Rock Titan, the Lava Titan, the Ice Titan, the Tornado Titan, and the one-eyed Cyclops as they emerged from the pit.

“Good answer!” Hades replied gleefully. Then he sent the Cyclops on a special mission to Thebes to hunt down Hercules and destroy him.

Hermes was napping peacefully on a cloud when a loud rumbling shook him awake. His eyes flew open to see the angry Titans approaching Mount Olympus.

"Uh-oh!" he said to himself. "We're in big trouble!"

He raced to tell Zeus, who ordered him to summon the gods for an immediate counterattack. Hephaestus hammered lightning bolts as weapons, and the other gods prepared themselves for battle. But the gods were no match for the Tornado Titan, who sucked them up like a vacuum cleaner.

In the meantime, down on Earth, Thebes was in flames. The people cried out for Hercules to save them as the Cyclops went on a rampage, leaving destruction in his path.

Though he no longer possessed his strength, Hercules confronted the Cyclops, who kicked him across the street like a pebble. Meg pleaded with Hercules not to fight the giant, but Hercules no longer cared what happened to him. Then Meg heard a familiar whinnying coming from a nearby stable. She discovered Pegasus and untied him, and the two set off in search of Phil. Meg believed that only Phil could get through to Hercules.

When they found him, Phil was about to board a boat leaving Thebes.

"Hercules gave us something we'd both lost—hope!" Meg reminded him. "Now he's lost his hope! If you don't help him now, he'll die!" Hearing these words, Phil agreed to return to the city with her.

Up on Mount Olympus, Zeus was in trouble. All of the gods had been captured, and now he was out of lightning bolts.

"Hades!" exclaimed Zeus when the god of the Underworld appeared. "I should have known you were behind this!"

Then the Lava Titan arrived and surrounded Zeus with molten rock. To finish the job, the Ice Titan cooled the lava with his frigid breath. Zeus was soon encased in solid rock, unable to move.

Hercules was faring no better. When Phil and Meg found him, it was clear the Cyclops would finish him off in no time.

"C'mon, kid, fight back!" Phil pleaded. He encouraged Hercules not to lose sight of his dreams—or his belief in himself.

Hearing his words, Hercules' resolve returned. He grabbed a burning stick and thrust it at the monster's eye. The monster screamed and dropped Hercules.

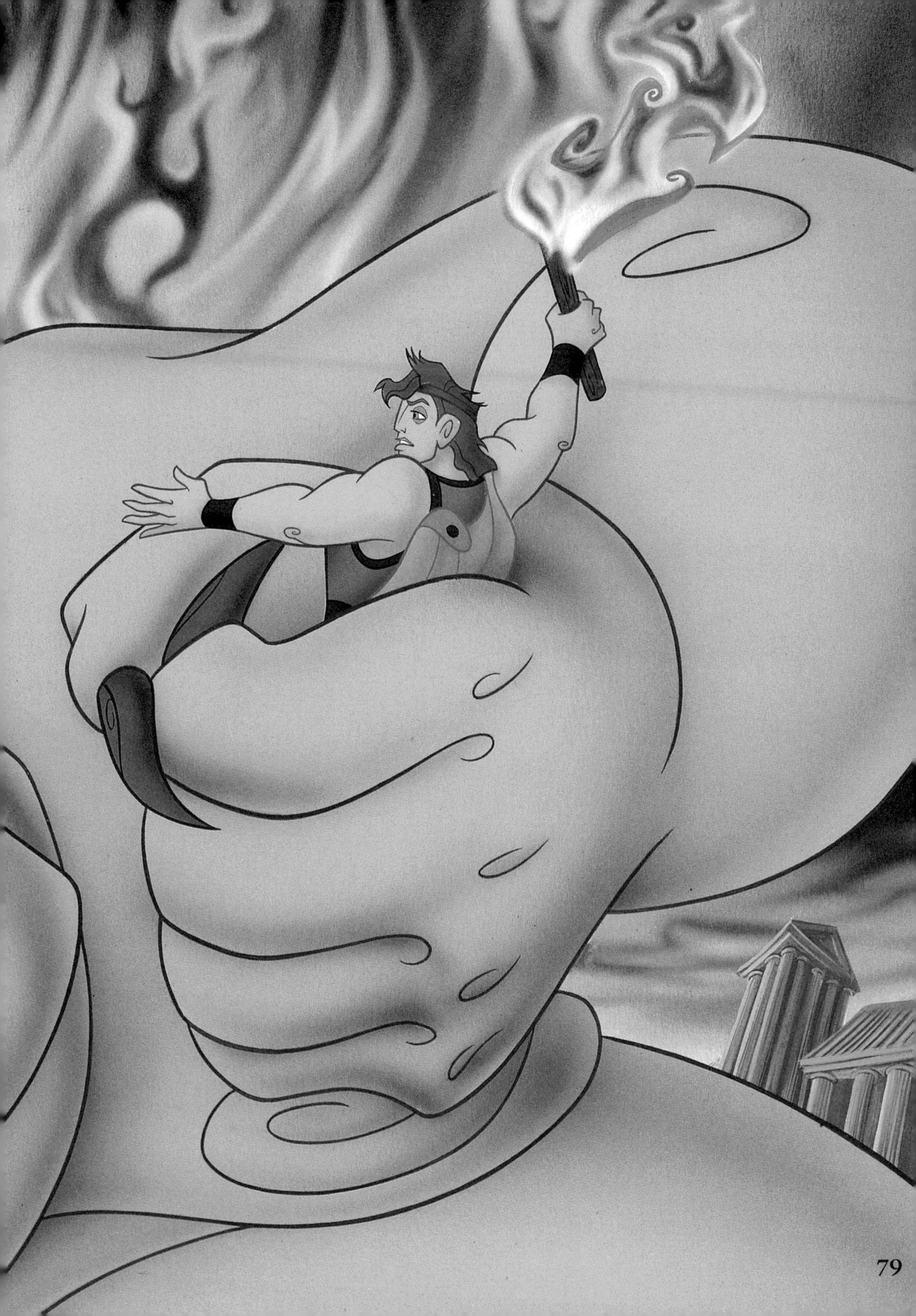

The Cyclops staggered over a cliff. Just then, a column the Cyclops had hit fell toward Hercules. Meg pushed him out of the way, so she was pinned instead. As Hercules tried to lift the pillar, his strength returned. “Hades’ deal is broken,” Meg explained weakly. “He promised I wouldn’t get hurt. You must go to Olympus and stop him.” Before he left her side, Meg finally admitted to Hercules that she loved him.

Hercules swept up to Mount Olympus, breaking the chains that bound the gods. Then, with his bare hands, he broke apart the lava that imprisoned his father, Zeus. Hephaestus rushed to fashion a new supply of lightning bolts, and the gods went back on the attack. Zeus and Hercules joined forces. Zeus's lightning bolts held the Titans back while Hercules used the Tornado Titan to swoop them up. Then Hercules hurled the Titans into space.

Knowing his plan was ruined, Hades started to make his getaway. "Thanks a ton, Wonder Boy," Hades began. "But I got one swell consolation prize. A friend of yours who's dying to see me."

Horrified, Hercules realized that Hades meant Meg.

Hercules raced back to her side, but it was too late. The Fates had cut Meg's Thread of Life.

"This wasn't supposed to happen!" Hercules cried in anguish.

"I'm sorry, kid," Phil said sadly. "But there are some things you can't change."

A look of determination came over Hercules' face. "Yes, I can," he replied as he mounted Pegasus once more.

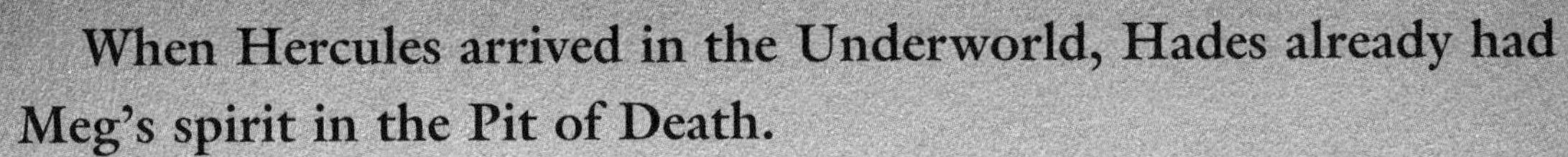

When Hercules arrived in the Underworld, Hades already had Meg's spirit in the Pit of Death.

"You like making deals," Hercules said. "Take me in Meg's place."

This was an unexpected bonus, Hades thought. "Okay!" he agreed. "You get her out...she goes—you stay!"

Hercules dived into the Pit of Death to retrieve Meg's spirit, growing older and older until it was clear he was near death himself. But when the Fates tried to cut his Thread of Life, they were shocked to find that they could not.

Hercules carried Meg's spirit out of the pit.

"You can't be alive!" cried Hades. "You'd have to be a…a…"

"A god?" Pain and Panic offered helpfully.

Hades tried to smooth things over. "You and Zeus can take a little joke, right?" he asked. Hercules ignored him. Then Hades reached out to Meg's spirit and pleaded, "Meg! Meg, talk to him!"

That was enough! With a mighty fist, Hercules hurled Hades down into the Pit of Death. The spinning spirits of the dead dragged the lord of the Underworld down into their ghostly midst.

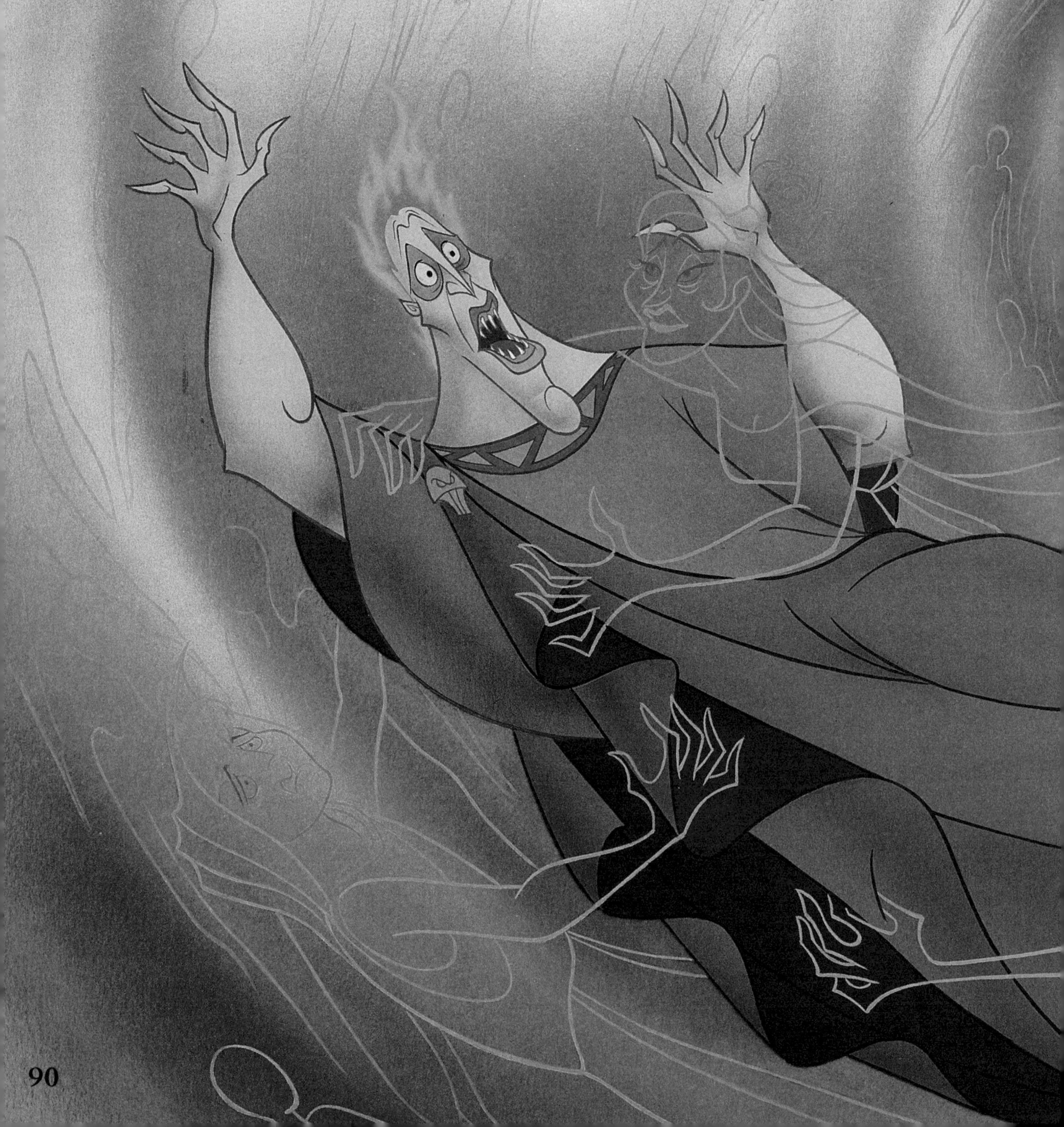

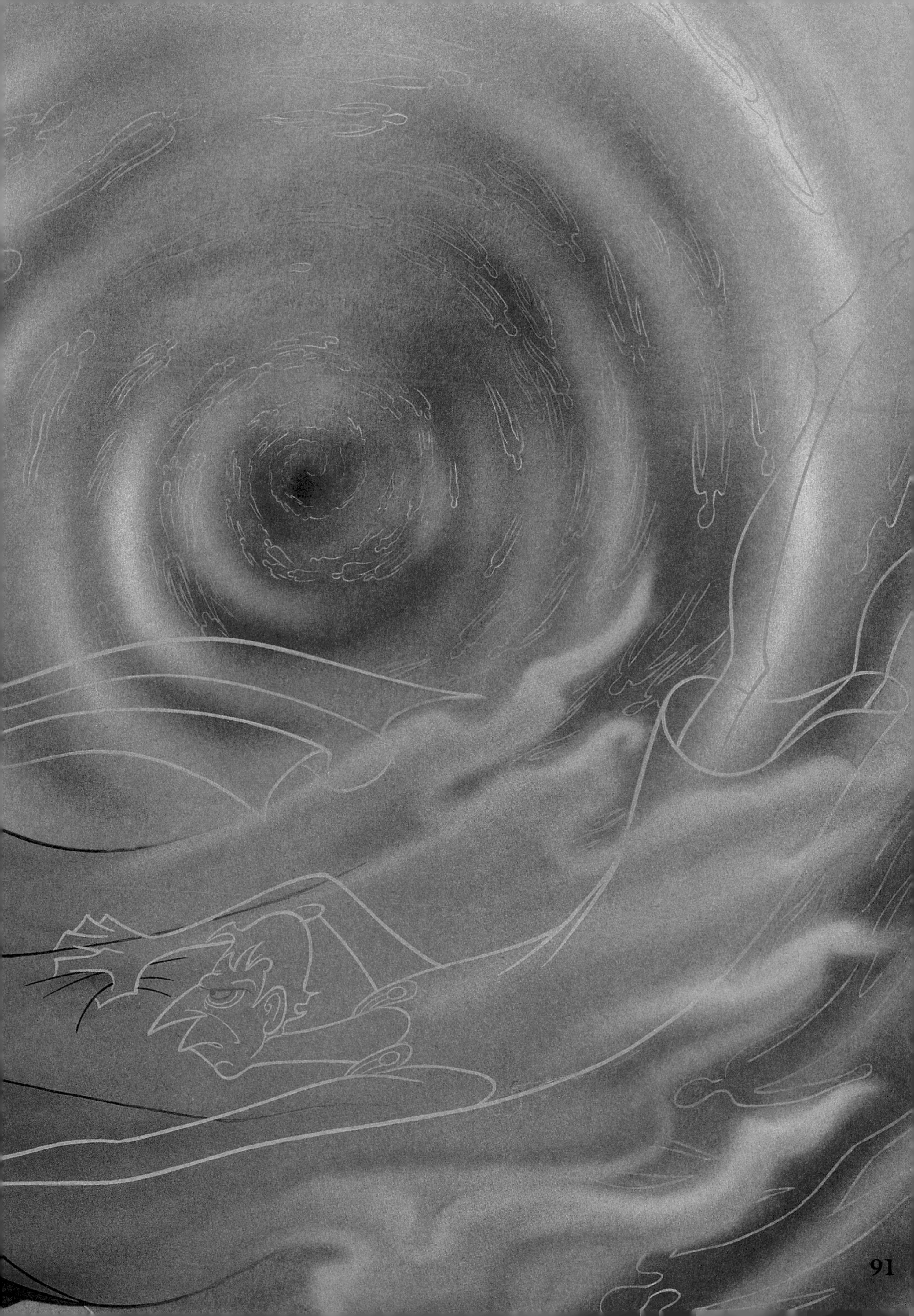

Hercules carried Meg's spirit back to her body. As soul and flesh reunited, her eyes fluttered open. She was alive! While Hercules and Meg held each other tight, Zeus lifted them to Mount Olympus on a cloud.

"A true hero isn't measured by the size of his strength, but by the strength of his heart," Zeus proclaimed. "Welcome home, Son!"

"Father, this is the moment I've always dreamed of," Hercules began. "But a life without Meg—even an immortal one—would be empty. I wish to stay on Earth with her. I finally know where I belong."

Zeus looked at Hera, who nodded her approval.

They would miss him, but Zeus and Hera knew that Hercules had found happiness at last. Their beloved son returned to a hero's welcome on Earth. In the cheering crowd were Herc's earthly parents, Alcmene and Amphitryon. Then someone pointed up to the sky, and everyone gazed in wonder at the constellation Zeus had created in his son's honor.

That is how the story ends—full of love and mirth.
Hercules was now a star in the heavens and on Earth.
And his friend Philoctetes at last had found a youth
Whose picture the gods put up in lights—and that's the gospel truth!